The Adventures of the Little Red Lipstick

Lolly Makes New Friends!

Christina Ann Zaremba

To order additional copies of this book, contact:
Xlibris
844-714-8691
www.Xlibris.com
Orders@Xlibris.com

ISBN: Softcover   978-1-6698-1468-9
        Hardcover   978-1-6698-1469-6
        EBook   978-1-6698-1467-2

Print information available on the last page

Rev. date: 05/13/2022

The Adventures of the Little Red Lipstick
Lolly Makes New Friends!

The department store was all a-buzz when word got out that the shipment of Serene Starr's new lipstick collection had just arrived that morning. All the Beauty Specialists from Serene Starr's Counter were running around, frantically cleaning and clearing a new space for the lipsticks. Harold, the store manager, dropped off a huge box at the counter. The ladies had a few minutes before the store meeting to unbox and display the new lipsticks. The store would open in just one hour!

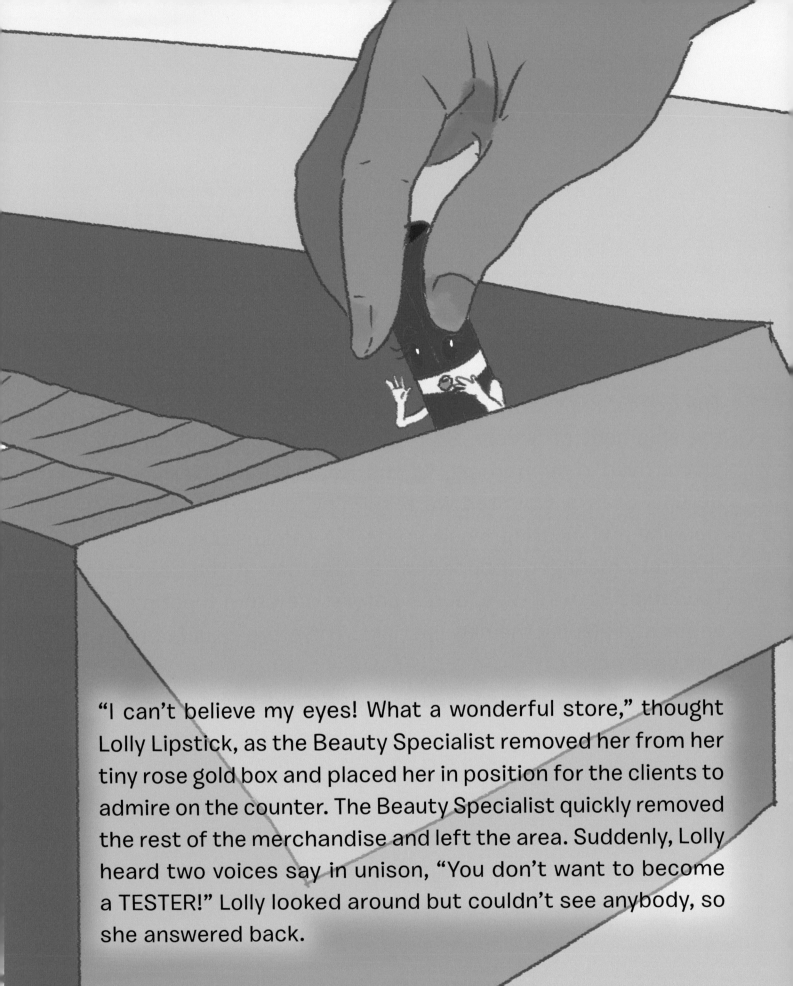

"I can't believe my eyes! What a wonderful store," thought Lolly Lipstick, as the Beauty Specialist removed her from her tiny rose gold box and placed her in position for the clients to admire on the counter. The Beauty Specialist quickly removed the rest of the merchandise and left the area. Suddenly, Lolly heard two voices say in unison, "You don't want to become a TESTER!" Lolly looked around but couldn't see anybody, so she answered back.

"Excuse me," Lolly asked, looking around the shiny rose gold boxes she was surrounded by. The voices said in unison again: "You don't want to become a Tester!"

"Who are you?" asked Lolly.

"Our names are Bella and Donna, Belladonna Eyelashes! We are twin sisters!" said the duo in unison, as they walked around the rose gold boxes and presented themselves to Lolly.

"Oh hi, my name is Lolly, Lolly Lipstick," Lolly said in a friendly voice.

"What does it mean to be a tester?" She asked with a worried look.

"It means that you get tried on all day by different people! They test the color on the back of their hand or wrist to see if the color will look good on them. Just look at poor Lacey Lipstick over there," Donna said, pointing to a worn-out lipstick on display. Poor Lacey looked exhausted!

"Yesterday she had been in the clutches of a young girl who was role-playing movie star makeup," said Bella. Hot pink lipstick was not only on the little girl's lips but on her eyes, cheeks, and chin, too. Her mother, who was blissfully getting her makeup done paid no attention to what the little girl was doing. The only time Lacey Lipstick felt better was when her head was dipped in alcohol and wiped clean of germs.

"Oh, dear! What should I do?" asked Lolly.

"We can hide you," said Bella and Donna in unison, giving each other a sneaky look. "We know the perfect place too!"

"Oh! Can you?" cried Lolly.

"Sure, what are friends for?" giggled Bella and Donna, eyeing each other again. "All you have to do is jump into the bottom drawer when the Beauty Specialist opens it. No one will ever find you there!"

"But then what will happen to me? Will I ever get to go home with someone?" Lolly asked worriedly. "I have big dreams of a famous movie star buying me one day! I'll get to go to red carpet events and ride around in a fancy purse all day long!"

"Hmph! The chances of that ever happening are slim to none," chimed in Bella and Donna as they rolled their eyes.

As Lolly and the twins were having their conversation, Madame Mascara strolled by and interrupted their conversation. "Pardon me my little one," Madame Mascara said as she stopped in front of Lolly. "Don't pay any attention to those two. They are in constant competition with one another and only care about themselves."

"Uh, I don't understand Ma'am...," said Lolly.

"It's Madame Mascara, darling!" said Madame.

"Uh yes, Madame, I was worried about becoming a tester," said Lolly, clearing her throat. "Can that really happen?"

"Darling, anything can happen, but let me put your mind at ease! You will not become a tester simply because when the sales lady pulled you out of the box she did not place a label on you that reads 'TESTER', therefore you are safe," explained Madame Mascara.

"Oh WOW! I can relax then?"

"Not really, darling! Here at this department store we always have to be at our best! Especially if we want someone to buy us," replied Madame Mascara. Bella and Donna sauntered over and wedged in between Lolly and Madame. "Hahaha! The Beauty Specialist didn't have time to put a tester label on any of the new lipsticks that arrived," smirked Bella and Donna. Lolly looked worried once again.

"Ooh-la-la, mon a mi! You are a part of the new lipstick collection, no?" asked a gorgeous pearly pink powder puff. Her outer presentation was that of a fancy rose gold compact, adorned with silver stars that sparkled like diamonds. "Do not pay any attention to Bella and Donna...they only wish to harm you!"

Madame Mascara interrupted them both saying, "May I present Mademoiselle Powder Puff! Meet Lolly Lipstick." Lolly shook hands with Mademoiselle Powder Puff and continued to ask questions.

"What would the twins gain by harming me?" Lolly asked the beautiful powder puff.

The twins turned around with anger in their voices and said, "We are right here, so stop talking about us like we aren't! We were only trying to help poor little lipstick not become a tester. What's wrong with that?" said Bella and Donna together.

"Shhh! Someone is coming," said Madame Mascara. Everyone scrambled to their spots unnoticed.

The Beauty Specialist came up to the counter and placed a lip-gloss and bronzer next to Lolly and Madame and walked away.

"Phew! That was close," exclaimed Lolly with relief, as she clutched her heart. Suddenly, she heard an unfamiliar voice that sounded sweet.

"They can never see us move or we will become frozen just like plain old makeup – never to speak again! By the way, my name is Lola Lip Gloss, and this is my boyfriend Bo Bronzer. We are inseparable," Lola said with a giggle, as she hugged Bo tightly and kissed him on the cheek.

"Bronzer and lip gloss look good together," said Bo with a wink. Lolly turned to Lola and asked, "What does it mean when we turn into plain old makeup?"

"You sure do have a lot to learn here before you go out in the real world, my love," said Bo Bronzer.

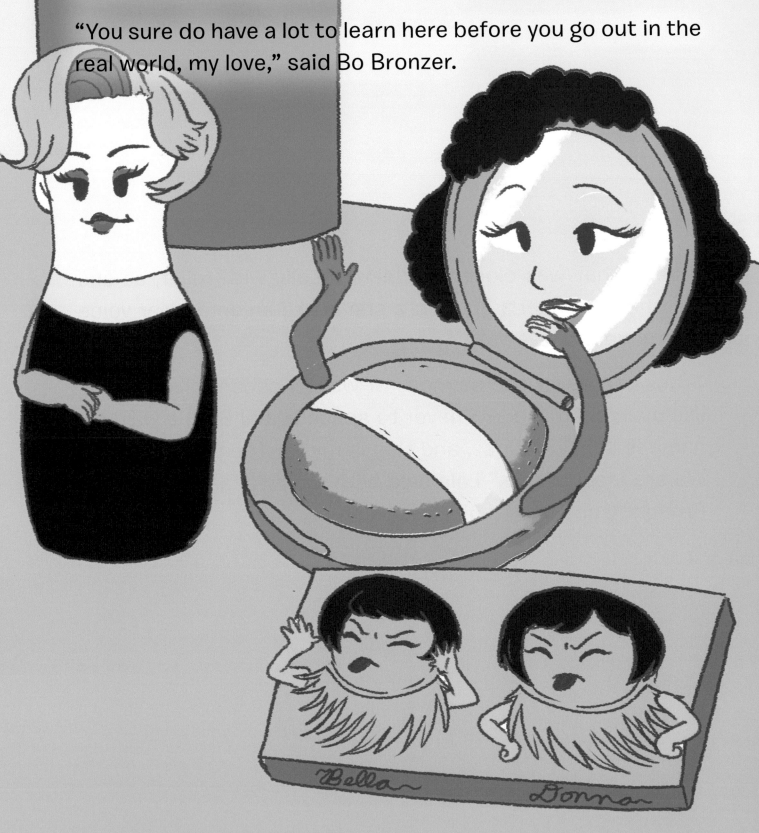

"Exactly" replied Mademoiselle Powder Puff.

"That's why we always stick together," exclaimed Bella and Donna.

"Hahaha, yeah right," said Bo, laughing sarcastically at the twins. Bella and Donna shot Bo an ugly glare and stuck out their tongues.

"Humans finding out about our secret is a big deal around here. If a human catches you moving around or even talking, you will permanently become frozen! FOREVER! No going back," said Bo Bronzer.

Lolly shuttered. Could this really happen, she wondered. Lolly couldn't think about that now. She was more concerned with not becoming a tester. Lolly turned to everyone and asked the dreaded question: "How can I make sure that I won't become a tester?"

Everyone huddled together and began whispering as Lolly waited for an answer. The first person to speak was Madame Mascara.

"We all decided that we must find somewhere to hide you until they put the tester label on one of the other lipsticks," explained Madame.

"It has to be a place where we have easy access," said Bo Bronzer.

"I've got it! How about we hide Lolly in the top drawer by the register," asked Lola Lip Gloss.

"Magnifique!" yelled Mademoiselle Powder Puff.

"We only have about 10 minutes until the Beauty Specialists come back," explained Madame Mascara, looking at the wall clock above the enormous swinging door.

"How should we get Lolly inside the drawer?" Bella and Donna asked together.

"We all need to work together," explained Lola Lip Gloss.

One by one, the friends joined hands and helped lower Lolly into the top drawer. Once inside, Lolly looked around and found a comfortable corner to hide until a new tester was put out on the counter. Lolly let out a sigh of relief and thought about her exciting day and all the new friends she had met. As she drifted off to sleep, she began to dream about what wonderful things awaited her tomorrow...

Printed in the United States
by Baker & Taylor Publisher Services